I Want a Shop!

Licensed by The Illuminated Film Company
Based on the LITTLE PRINCESS animation series © The Illuminated Film Company 2008
Made under licence by Andersen Press Ltd., London
'I Want a Shop!' episode written by Dan Wicksman.
Producer Iain Harvey. Director Edward Foster.
© The Illuminated Film Company/Tony Ross 2008
Design and layout © Andersen Press Ltd, 2008.
Printed and bound in China by C&C Offset Printing.
10   9   8   7   6   5   4   3   2   1
British Library Cataloguing in Publication Data available.

ISBN: 978 1 84270 762 3 (Trade edition)
ISBN: 978 1 84939 702 5 (Riverside Books edition)

I Want a Shop!

Tony Ross

Andersen Press · London

Back at the castle, the Little Princess had a marvellous idea. "I'm going to have my own shop!" She raced up to her bedroom to find some things to sell.

The Little Princess rummaged in her toy box, then picked out a
dolly. "I can't sell that," she decided. "I might want to play with it."
She looked at everything, then put everything back.
"I need to find other things to sell instead."

The Little Princess pushed her pram along the castle corridor.
"What's this?"
She picked a wooden box off the table and gave it a shake.

WWwHHhhheeeeeeeeEE!!!!

A jack-in-the-box sprung out. "Ooohhh!"
gasped the Little Princess. "I could sell this." As nobody was
using the jack-in-the-box, she tossed it into the pram.

The castle was full of things that nobody was using. In the Gardener's shed, she found three lovely pots.

In the Chef's kitchen cupboards, she discovered an interesting bowl with holes in it.

The castle living room had even more treasures.
The Little Princess started with the King's old train set.
"He's too big to play with it now," she decided.

"Woah, girl!" commanded the General, when he spotted Scruff's arrow. "Well, this looks jolly interesting."
He quickly re-mounted Nessie and cantered inside.

The Little Pri

hadn't thoug

"It's yours for

The General

"It's a deal!"

No one could resist the Little Princess's sign.

"Is it a treasure hunt?" grinned the Admiral, taking out his

telescope. Scruff wagged his tail and spun round. Standing still

is difficult for dogs.

"Look, Dad!" she called. "You can do a magic trick with these pots!" The King was so impressed, he bought the pots in exchange for promising to tell the Little Princess a story later.

The Genera
"Err…" paus
"I'll take it!"

"Princess!" frowned the Chef. "I do
not want to buy a choo choo train."
"But it will make things come to you,"
said the Little Princess.
She sent the salt and pepper
up the track and sold him
the train in seconds.

Scruff's sign tempted the Gardener in for a browse. "Do you have anything to keep those pesky rabbits off my vegetables?" The Little Princess reached for her jack-in-the-box.

"I've got just the thing."

"I'll take it!" chuckled the Gardener. "And I'll give you some strawberries in return."

The Little Princess grinned. By the time she'd sold a windmill to the Prime Minister, her shop was nearly sold out.

"Hello!" called the Prime Minister, speeding outside on his trike.

The Gardener and the King
looked very cross.
"They're my plant pots!"
shouted the Gardener.
The King shook his head.
"I bought this trick at the
Princess's shop!"

The General trotted over,
then suddenly pulled up
in front of the
Prime Minister.
"That's my windmill!"

"Nobody likes my shop," sniffed the Little Princess.
Now she wouldn't get a ride on Nessie, a long story, a trike ride,
or any of the other things she had been promised!

Over the other side of the garden, the
Prime Minister did something very special.
"Gardener, you need this more than me."
The Gardener looked down at the
jack-in-the-box and beamed.

The Prime Minister's kind gesture gave the King an idea.
"Maybe we should all swap back?"
Everyone passed back their shopping, then set out to find
the Little Princess.

"We've decided that we should keep what we bought," explained the King. The Little Princess gasped. **"Really?"** "Yes," said the General. "So we've all come to pay you!"

The Little Princess's shop had earned her all sorts of wonderful treats. It had been an afternoon of stories, horse-play and trike rides.

"Princess!" sang the Chef. "We 'ave your cakes!"

"And your strawberries," added the Gardener.

"Yummy!" cheered the Little Princess. "But there are so many…"
Suddenly she burst into giggles.

"...I can sell them in my shop!"

Look out for more Little Princess TV tie-ins:

Little Princess Castle Playtime — Activity Book

Little Princess Round and Round the Garden — Sticker Book — As Seen on TV

Little Princess Fun in the Sun! — Activity Book — As Seen on TV

Little Princess I Want to Do Magic! — Sticker Book — As Seen on TV

Little Princess I Want My Tent!

Little Princess Can I Keep it? — As Seen on TV

Little Princess I Don't Want to Comb My Hair! — As Seen on TV

Little Princess I Want a Trumpet! — As Seen on TV

Little Princess I Want My New Shoes! — As Seen on TV

Little Princess I Want a Shop! — As Seen on TV

Little Princess I Want to Go to the Fair! — As Seen on TV

Little Princess I Don't Like Salad! — As Seen on TV

Little Princess I Want My Sledge! — As Seen on TV

Little Princess I Don't Want a Cold! — As Seen on TV

www.andersenpress.co.uk
www.littleprincesskingdom.com

When the Little Princess decides to open her own shop, it's a roaring success! The King and his courtiers are soon queuing up to buy the ingenious objects on her stall. But when the happy customers meet later and compare goods, the Little Princess has some explaining to do…

ISBN 978-1-84939-702-5

UK £4.99   www.andersenpress.co.uk

9 781849 397025